Petey and the Mean Pirates

By Donna Mirsky Bennett * Pictures By J.C. Mull

D1530652

This book is dedicated to Sean, Cady, Sam, and Rachel for showing me my true purpose in life – to be a nice pirate aboard this swashbuckling ship we call home. Every day, we add a little bit of color to each other's lives.

First American Edition 2008
New York

Text and illustrations copyright 2008, Donna Mirsky Bennett and J.C. Mull

Printed in New York by Three Chiquitas Publishing
http://www.threechiquitaspublishing.com
threechiquitas@att.net

1 2 3 4 5 6 7 8 9 10

ISBN 9780615229546

Petey and the Mean Pirates

By Donna Mirsky Bennett * Pictures By J.C. Mull

Petey was different. You could tell just by looking at him.

He was the youngest one on the ship, but there was something else………

He was actually nice! Usually, being nice was a good thing, (but, not if you're supposed to be a pirate!)

Petey lived aboard a ship full of very mean and scary pirates. It was okay – Petey liked them. They were his friends. It's just that sometimes he wondered why he was on this ship with all of these mean pirates in the first place.

It was hard to be friends with them. They kept getting mad at him for being so nice all the time.

One day, Petey and his shipmates snuck on board another ship so they could steal treasures. All the mean pirates from his ship yelled, "AAARGH!" They waved their swords around at the other guys and made them walk the plank.

Petey watched all of this and knew he should at least TRY to be mean. So, he walked up to one of the guys from the other ship and started to look him in the eye with a scary look. But, then he felt a smile spread over his face and he heard himself say, "Hi! My name's Petey. How are you doing? Nice day, huh?"

The next thing you know, Petey was sitting down playing cards with his new friend whose name, incidentally, was Jim. Petey's brother's name was Jim, too! So, you see, they had something to talk about! Petey and Jim sat like this amongst all of the swashbuckling. They ate chips and drank juice drinks with fancy umbrellas in them until they heard Captain Carl yelling,

"PETEY!!!!! What on EARTH are you doing????"

Captain Carl was very mad. He just had a talk with Petey last week about not being mean enough! So, Petey politely excused himself and went back to the mean pirate ship.

The pirates had a talk with Petey (again) and asked him why he was having such a hard time being mean. "The scarier we are," Captain Carl and his mates reasoned, "the more treasures we'll get and the richer we'll be!"

"It's hard," said Petey. "I know you want me to be like you and I like hanging out here. You are my friends. But every time I try to be mean, a smile comes over my face and I just feel like getting someone else to smile, too." He looked around at their faces and they were not smiling. They were angry with him. So Petey told them he'd try again tomorrow.

That night, Petey tossed and turned in his hammock. His mother and father had always taught him and his brother to be nice. How did he get himself mixed up with these pirates? How did he end up on this ship? Was there some reason he was here???

He tossed and turned so much that he fell right out onto the floor. Then he realized there was a huge storm, so he went up on the deck to help out. He liked life at sea. One day it was sunny and calm, and the next was a raging storm like this one.

The waves crashed up on the deck and threw the ship all around. There was wind. And rain. And lightning. And thunder.

Suddenly, the whole ship tilted on its side. The pirates battled the waves and tried to get their ship straight up again, but it was useless. It capsized and Petey and all the mean pirates found themselves floating in the cold, dark ocean, watching the fierce waves destroy their home.

Just when they thought it couldn't get any worse, Captain Carl yelled something, but it was hard to hear him because he was trying to stay afloat and hold on to his treasure chest at the same time.

"WHAT????" Petey yelled back.

"I said………SHARKS!!!!!!!!!" Captain Carl screamed.

The mean pirates did all that they knew how to do. They yelled, "AARGH!" at the sharks and tried poking at them with their swords. Nothing worked. The sharks were hungry and swords don't work on hungry sharks!

Petey looked down at the shark who was just about to eat him and said with a smile, "Can you believe this storm?"

The shark looked Petey right in the eye and answered, "No. You know, it was sunny and warm just a few hours ago!"

Petey said, "Well look, we've had a pretty rough night, so I was wondering if you'd be able to just let me and my friends go?"

The shark looked at HIS friends, though, and said, "Well, I'd like to but we're all pretty hungry. We kind of need to eat......YOU!"

"I see. Do you live around here?" asked Petey.

"Yes," the shark answered. He was pointing with his fin. "Just over there."

"What do you say we go back to your place, find you sharks some jewels and gold from Captain Carl's treasure chest, and we can all hang out and eat ice cream?" Petey suggested.

So, they did just that. Captain Carl was willing to give up some jewels since he was just happy to be alive. And, from that day forward, Petey was put in charge of negotiations and communications with oncoming ships (and sharks).

Petey and the mean pirates built themselves a new ship and lived happily ever after. Plus, they learned that sharks really REALLY love mint chocolate chip ice cream!

Vocabulary Section

Capsize – Tip over. The boat **capsized** and all the pirates fell out into the ocean.

Negotiate – A way to talk to people to make sure you get what you want and they get what they want. Petey was the one to **negotiate** with the sharks so they could stay alive and eat ice cream together.

Communicate - Talking and having conversations with others. Petey liked to **communicate** with other people….and sharks!

Swashbuckling – Wild play and roughhousing, usually with pirates and swords. Petey and Jim played cards while the other pirates were **swashbuckling**.

Discussion Questions

1. Did being rich and having a treasure chest filled with jewels and gold help Captain Carl against the sharks? Why or why not?

2. Did yelling, "AAARGH!" and using swords help the pirates fight the sharks? Please explain.

3. Why do you think the pirates were able to become friends with the sharks?

4. Do you think Petey should stay with the mean pirates? Why or why not?

5. Do you think Petey and the mean pirates should try to do something else with their new ship, or should they continue being pirates?